COST OF
FREEDOM II

KATHERINE
ZARTMAN

Lavender Moon Publishing

Lavender Moon Publishing

ISBN: 978-0-578-23397-0

PRINTED IN THE UNITED STATES OF AMERICA

CHAPTER ONE

Lars and I drive home with expected desires for a life without the weekly visits to the VA. Will the pills and my compassion chase away the PTSD and self-loathing that Lars confronts, fade them into the past, and open the door to a new life?

We hold hands and talk about the future possibilities of life together. The cold, dark house is soon bright, and a warm, crackling fire ignites in us and the fireplace. I get up and gather a few blankets and pillows as Lars drops his crutch and pushes a side table close enough for support. Lowering his body carefully to avoid a fall, he is soon horizontal and gestures for me to join him. I kiss him and whisper, "I will get us some wine to aid our celebration." I open a bottle of wine, gather glasses, and add them to a spacious tray. We both take a few sips of the cold, sweetly spiced blend of California grapes.

Lars reaches over with his right hand and strokes my breasts. "Are you warm enough? I want to take your top off."

I answer him by pulling my thermal shirt over my head and kissing him. "It's going to be good, baby." He pulls me closer to him, and I feel his warmth and a growing erection pressing against my thigh. Lars shifts his weight, and when stable, he lowers his cool lips to my breast. Pulling on the nipple, he drags his right hand downward and releases the waistband of my jeans. A loud pop from the fireplace startles us, and we pause for a wine sip. I tease Lars and tell him we should probably dress in case of a fire. "Oh baby, the only fire will be in you when I take you."

I kiss him and explore the tongue and smooth teeth I know so well. He returns my efforts and then breaks contact, his hand returning to my jeans and lips back to a breast. "God Arlene, I love you so much. You have made me a man again." Then he smiles and says, "Almost."

I kiss the stump of his left arm and run my fingers over the stump of his right leg. Lars jerks in pain as I caress the end of his stump. "Easy baby, easy. I love you, Lars, but we need to see Dr. Todd about a revision. You should not continue to have nerve pain, and I think a prosthesis will really help your mobility."

Lars struggles to sit up, kisses me, and tells me, "You know how I feel about that. I'm scared, Arlene."

I kiss Lars and tell him, "We just need to find out what Dr. Todd thinks and then decide what to do. You can always say no, Lars. I am with you for whatever you decide. Now, stop worrying and let me play with you." I ease his sweatpants down, kiss his stump and then take him in my mouth.

Lars grunts and says, "Just a taste—I want to come inside you, baby."

"Yes Lars, I want that too." I shift, still holding him tightly between my lips as I push my jeans all the way down. I use my feet to completely pull them off, knowing Lars cannot do it without my help. Having only one hand complicates the most mundane tasks. Pulling a blanket over us, I guide his member and he whispers, "Home, sweet home."

CHAPTER TWO

We continue to discuss the surgery and I point out the positives possible if Lars has a revision. After telling him how nice it would be if we could take our dog (not here yet) for walks and take a trip to Norway to visit his country and family, Lars relents, and I make an appointment.

On the phone with Dr. Todd, I explain Lars's resistance to revising the stump.

"Arlene," Dr. Todd starts, "you know I won't be able to guarantee Lars that I won't have to take more of the leg. We will just have to see, but I will do the absolute best I can."

"I know you will, Dr. Todd, and I will be there to navigate his rehab and support his anxiety no matter what."

"Arlene, you are such a special nurse. You understand these poor men and what anguish they live with."

"I know, Dr. Todd. I live with their tortured thoughts and bodies, and I have a functional blindness to not see the damages of war. We will see you in two weeks, Dr. Todd; go save a few limbs."

Later in the day, I spend hours with Lars, perusing rescue dogs on the computer, and we find a rescue for huskies about two hundred miles away. Lars wants to go right away, but I rein in his enthusiasm by reminding him that we can't take care of a dog yet as he will have surgery and rehab first, and that it could possibly be months before we can adopt a dog. He is disappointed but understands that some dreams must wait.

We go to Dr. Todd and he is rather positive upon examining Lars's stump. He notes where the nerves fire and the roughness of the bone ends, telling Lars that it will likely be a month in the hospital following surgery but that he thinks Lars will have a positive outcome. Surgery is scheduled and we spend the night before holding tightly to each other. He rolls over and enters me, frantically pumping, fast and furious, but is unable to climax. "I'm sorry, baby. I can't, I can't."

"Oh Lars, you are just too worried; roll over and let me help you."

Lars turns to me and I take him in my mouth, swirl my tongue on the head and suck hard. "Fuck! I'm going to come already, baby!"

"Let it go, Lars; let it go," I garble and with a final jerk, he explodes in my mouth. "Thank God, I needed that."

"I love you, Lars. Don't worry—I will be with you all the way."

"Arlene, you are the best narcotic I can take."

"Yes Lars, and I won't cause you constipation, either." I chuckle. He grimaces, remembering the impaction procedure I had to do on him. I kiss his eyes and tell him to sleep.

"You need to rest for tomorrow." I massage his shoulders and soon his breathing changes. "Good night, Lars. I love you; sleep well."

CHAPTER THREE

I wake Lars at 5:00 a.m., help him to dress and we head to the VA. Surgery is scheduled for 6:00 a.m., and we are directed to pre-surgery for prep. I get Lars changed into a gown and Linda, a surgical nurse, comes to start an IV, take vitals, and explain that the doctor will be in soon.

Dr. Todd comes in and marks the stump and tells Linda to inject the medication that will make Lars sleepy. I pull up the gown on Lars and grab some antibacterial wipes to ensure he is free of bacteria prior to surgery. I kiss him and tell him that I will see him soon and to close his eyes and go to sleep.

It has been three hours since the start of surgery when Dr. Todd comes over to talk to me, his surgical smock covered with blood, giving me the indication that surgery is not going well. He takes my hand, telling me that he only has a moment before he must return to Lars. He quickly relates he had to take a few inches from the stump and remove a lot of scar tissue, but he anticipates that Lars should have a good outcome. "Reassure him, Arlene; I'll see you in recovery in a few hours." He turns and hurries back to the surgical suite.

God. Just what Lars has feared the most. He will need me when he wakes and I can easily help with the drains and dressings, but I will have to tell the nurses that his PTSD needs to be confronted.

Dr. Todd finishes and returns to explain what he has done and what to expect. "Lars is in recovery. Give him a few hours and then you can see him."

I hate being restricted, but I am no longer a nurse here and must rely on others. When I am finally able to see Lars, I kiss him and lift his gown to see if blood is visible. I know he will want to look at the stump. Lars is mumbling and waking up, so I pull a chair over to his bedside, hold his hand tightly, and wait for full cognition. Big blue eyes slowly open and he wants to know how the surgery went. I hesitate, not sure what I should tell him, knowing his aversion to the shortening of his stump.

"Lars, Dr. Todd is pleased with the surgery. He removed lots of scar tissue and removed the rough ends of the stump. Your leg is two inches shorter but will be pain-free."

Lars panics and pulls the sheet down to see the stump, but I stop him as I do not want him to see the dressing, fearing it will trigger a PTSD attack. I kiss him, walk around to the other side of the bed, lower the guardrail and scrunch up to Lars in the bed. Strictly not allowed but oh, so needed. I pull Lars to my chest and smooth his blond hair, kissing his neck where his pulse is rapidly jerking around. He gradually calms and soon he drifts off. God, I love this fragile man.

I kiss his forehead and move to the chair to wait while he sleeps. A nurse comes in to take vitals, so I tell her I am a former nurse from this hospital and that I will help Lars with his dressing changes, bathroom, and showers. "Can I check the computer for orders and meds?"

"Absolutely not," she responds. "You can help with care but no access to his orders. You will have to talk to Dr. Todd."

Lars mumbles, tries to sit up and pull the sheet back. I pull the sheet back down and push down the guardrails on the bed. "Do you have pain, baby?"

"Yeah, my leg is throbbing."

"Okay. I'll see if I can get you some meds." I am worried that Lars has so much pain so soon after surgery, so I tell the nurse to call Dr. Todd and explain. He comes in a few minutes later and tells me it is bone pain since he had to cut more back, and he will order meds immediately. The nurse leaves and returns in a few minutes with the meds—strong ones. I hope this does not continue long as with these particular meds, Lars could become constipated and perhaps impacted again. I make sure he has lots of water to drink and return to the chair, knowing that he will sleep for several hours. I nap for an hour, then get up to check Lars's vitals and pull a warm throw from the bag I packed prior to surgery. Why is it always so cold for patient visitors? It seems normal for the patient, with the nurses always warming blankets for them. Is it the anxiety and nerves of loved ones, watching while the patients recover?

I am praying for Lars when he wakes again, and I buzz the nurse for more pain medication. It will be several days of this before our pattern will change and Lars will be fully awake. When I see Dr. Todd later, I ask if

I can get a sofa in the room as I will be sleeping here until Lars is better.

"I'm breaking rules for you, Arlene, but you are worth it, as is Lars."

"Thank you, Dr. Todd. I appreciate your help since Lars is just so fragile." Maintenance comes half an hour later, bearing a small sofa, and I take another nap, knowing I will be on the same erratic schedule as Lars. A few hours later, I hear Lars moaning, and his Percocet arrives just in time. After the nurse leaves, I give Lars more water and an apple juice.

"I need the urinal, baby."

I go to the attached bathroom and bring the urinal to the bed for Lars. I place his cock in the urinal and he relieves himself. I note the number of CCs and dump the contents in the toilet. I wash my hands and return to Lars, curling up next to him with my arms around his waist.

"Just a few days of this, Lars, and you will feel much better."

"Baby, you should go home and rest."

"Lars, I am sleeping here; I won't leave you alone."

"Oh baby, I love you."

"I love you too, and I'm here. Are you afraid?"

"Yes," Lars says. "I want to see my stump."

"Maybe tomorrow; I just don't want to trigger an attack." I kiss him and tell him to sleep. He closes his eyes and I remain next to him for about an hour, but the bed guard is pressing into my back, so I return to the sofa. I close my eyes but wake when the nurse opens the door, the bright hall lights flooding into the room. She sets down some hot tea and applesauce for Lars just as he wakes and kisses, asking for water and a pill. This is just life for a post-op patient: meds, vitals, sleep, meds, vitals, sleep. "I need the urinal, baby."

The nurse leaves, letting us know that Dr. Todd will be in at eight. I fetch the urinal, again noting the CCs as he stops—seems like his kidneys are working well. I place the urinal in front of Lars again. "Just a few more CCs, Lars, and then I will give you some applesauce."

"I'm not hungry," he mumbles.

"I know, but you need to eat a little." He eats a few bites of the applesauce, then asks to see his stump. "Not until the drains are removed. We will see what Dr. Todd says. Now go back to sleep for a few hours."

I sip my tea, waiting for Lars to sleep so I can check the drains and his stump. The fluid is much less today, and the stump is looking much better. I pull the sheet back up and lie down to rest, waiting for Dr. Todd. When he does come, he checks the drains and tells me we can remove them and put a light dressing on the stump. Lars will be able to shower with a waterproof cover for the stump. With this good news, Dr. Todd orders a change in the meds, switching Lars to an injectable pain medication to help his bowels from binding.

"Make sure he eats, Arlene, and I'll order a saline drip as he is starting to bind."

"Thanks, Dr. Todd. I will take care of him."

CHAPTER FOUR

Lars sleeps for a few hours and I wake him when lunch arrives. He really does not want food, but I make him finish his lunch, even the chocolate pudding that was provided. I pull him up to a sitting position and he swings his leg and stump over the side. "My crutch."

"No, Lars, I won't risk a fall." I tell him to stand on his good leg and push up with his good arm. He is wobbly, so I get him down into the wheelchair, kiss him, and wheel him to the shower. Do you want the toilet?"

"Fuck no. Get this dressing off so I can see what I have left."

I get him up and transfer him to the shower seat. "Relax for a few minutes and I'll remove the dressing." I gather soap, a water-proof bag for the stump, shampoo, and his toothbrush and toothpaste.

"Here, Lars, brush your teeth so I can properly kiss you." I bend to unwrap the surgical dressing while he is distracted. "Close your eyes, Lars." I take his toothbrush and kiss him deeply, but he pulls away from me.

"Let me see; let me see," he insists.

"Keep your eyes closed until I tell you to open them." I remove the dressing and quickly fold it before placing it in the trash can for biomedical material.

"Can I open my eyes?" Lars asks.

"No, not yet. I just need to clean up the stump and then you can see it." I gently remove the residue with special wipes and toss them into the trash can.

"I'm cold, Arlene. Can you turn on the shower?"

"Not yet. I need to put on the waterproof bag and let you see the stump first. Okay, open your eyes, Lars, and look."

He opens his eyes and reaches to touch the end of the stump. "I can't see the end."

"Don't move. I'll get a mirror for you." I grab my compact and open it, holding it in position for Lars to see. The wound is dripping a little blood, so I tell him to close his eyes if it triggers an attack. He pushes my hand around to get the best angle for the mirror. He looks over the reflection and says, "Fuck, I can't handle this."

"Close your eyes, Lars." I pull a large towel over his shoulders and hug him tightly, pulling his head to my chest. He is shaking and tears run down his face. I squeeze him tighter, assuring him that we will get through this. His shaking gradually subsides, and he looks up at me. "Thank God you are here, Arlene; I need you. I am freezing. Will you put the stump cover on now and turn on the shower?"

With a nod, I quickly slide the waterproof bag over his stump and adjust the water temperature to warm up Lars. I think about removing my clothes but decide it is not proper for the hospital, so I just get wet. Water will not hurt me—just a pain to deal with. I soap up Lars and lather shampoo into his blond hair. Switching to the handheld shower nozzle, I rinse the soap from Lars's hair and body. I am dripping as I shut the water off. Lars begins to shiver, so I cover him with towels and wind a towel around my wet hair. "Sit still and I'll get your robe."

I pull his heavy robe from the closet and bend down to his legs and feet. Putting another towel on the shower floor, I tell Lars to stand and put his arm on my shoulder for support. I work the robe around him, feeding the stump of his left arm through the sleeve. He points out that he should probably be back in a hospital gown, but I smile.

"Lars, I am breaking so many rules that I will break another." I kiss him and transfer him to the wheelchair, pushing it to the bedside. I straighten the sheets and settle Lars into bed. I remove the bag on his stump and check for bleeding. He starts to relax, so I put a light dressing on the stump and page the nurses' station for a warm blanket. The nurse arrives, handing me the blanket, which I tuck securely around Lars. She also bears a cup of pain meds and watches Lars as he gratefully takes it.

Satisfied, his nurse says, "I need to put a new dressing on you, Lars."

I gently nudge her hand away, saying, "No need. I already cleaned and re-dressed the wound."

"Arlene," she says, smiling as she tries to sound stern. "You break the rules."

"Yes, I do, but I enjoy doing so," I smile back.

She leaves, and I make sure Lars is warm and comfortable before he nods off. "Sweet baby, you've had quite a morning." He drifts off and I retreat to the bathroom to change into clean clothes. I lie down, and just as sleep tries to overtake me, I suddenly hear, "Arlene, Arlene! I need the urinal!"

I jump up, startled, and bring the urinal to Lars. "I can do it," he says. "I need to stop acting like a baby."

"Oh Lars," I say sleepily, "you are all man and I love helping you with anything you need."

CHAPTER FIVE

The recovery from surgery continues, and we are both exhausted by the end of each day. As Lars's pain levels drop, we walk every morning and afternoon—Lars with his crutch rubbing blisters under his arms with the pressure. In the afternoons, we are in the gym for rehab, Lars working to regain some strength before he can go home.

We have resided in room 614 for a month, and now that the stitches are out and the stump is healing well, we are more than ready to go home. Dr. Todd checks in one morning and tells us, "One more week and you can go home. But you will have to continue rehab for several months, with at least five more months before we can consider fitting you with a prosthesis."

I kiss Lars and whisper, "One more week, baby," as he smiles back at me.

Finally, the week is over, and on our last morning, the staff brings discharge papers and outpatient instructions. I put our bags on the discharge cart and settle Lars into a wheelchair. Leaving him just outside the hospital entrance, I rummage through my purse for the keys as I walk to my car, hoping it will start. With a little persuasion, the car comes to life and I turn the heat up while I drive to pick up my love.

We are both happy to be leaving the hospital and anxious to be back home. I stop at the post office to pick up a staggering amount of mail that I had held for a month, then I make another stop at the grocery store as we need fresh food and a few supplies. I quickly get what we need, load the groceries into the car, and we head home. I get Lars inside, settle him in bed, and turn to go put away the groceries, but Lars pulls me to him and says, "Fuck the groceries—I want you now."

"Are you sure you feel strong enough?"

"Come over here and I'll show you how strong I am."

I kiss him and slide his sweatpants down. He is already hard and tells me to get naked. I do, and he whispers, "This won't last very long, but I need it now."

"I need it too, Lars," and I guide him to me. He grunts and frantically thrusts back and forth. He draws in a deep breath and releases it as he comes. "Oh baby, I love you so much. Thank you for taking such good care of me. I promise I will take care of you later."

"I'll make sure you do, Lars. Now, take a nap and I will put away the groceries. I'll make chili and cornbread for dinner."

I put the groceries away, start laundry and run the vacuum, then go through the mail and pay all the bills that need to be paid. I return to the bedroom and stretch out beside Lars, pulling him to me. He is warm and turns to me. Kissing me, he passionately tells me, "I love you, Arlene, I love you."

He trails his right hand down to my sex, but I stop the progress and tell him, "No, let's shower, and then you can show me how much." I support Lars and lead him to the shower. He sits on the shower chair as I slowly work suds over his shoulders, chest, and back, massaging as I knead his muscles. I clean myself as well, and Lars turns to me. "Can I help?"

"Sure," I smile. He brings his hand to my sex and twirls his fingers around my clitoris. Aroused, I turn to him and say, "There is one more muscle I need to massage." He spreads his legs, awaiting my touch while continuing with his hand on me. He starts to moan as I knead his most precious muscle, and he pulls me forward.

"Sit on me, baby, and let me come in you." I carefully maneuver onto his lap, and we rise and fall, rise and fall. We are both panting, and I clutch his shoulders as my orgasm explodes, his following seconds later. I collapse on his shoulder, and we just hold each other for several minutes as the warm water turns cooler. Eventually I turn the water off and help Lars out of the shower. I dry us both off and we stagger to the bed. I tell him, "I want more, and then I need to check the chili and finish the laundry."

He says, "Yeah, me too." I suck hard on him and he is soon ready for another session. "Hey, hey, slow down, baby—I want to make love to you, not just fuck." I roll him onto me, and we whisper endearments to each other. He moans softly as we finish together, then tells me, "Now I need to rest."

"Yes, sweet man, sleep. I love you." Lars is out very quickly, so I kiss his forehead and go to the kitchen. I add beans and a few fresh tomatoes to the chili, slice a few avocados, and put the wash in the dryer. I water a few plants and go into the living room to await Lars waking up. My eyes grow heavy and before I open them, I feel Lars kissing my neck. Surprised that he made his way into the living room on his own, I kiss him and tell him that dinner is almost ready. "Can we eat at the table?"

"Sure, let me set it, and I'll put the cornbread in the oven." Fifteen minutes later, I fill two bowls with the hot chili, adding some sour cream and avocado on top, and put the cornbread on a side plate. We eat together and talk about the future, walking our new dog, and our trip to Norway. I clear the table and we go into the library to peruse the husky rescue.

We find a white-and-silver puppy with blue eyes, and Lars says, "That's him; that's Sven." I look up at him and he says, "I want to call him Sven, after my dead brother. Do you mind?"

"It's perfect, Lars." I love the name, and it is Norwegian. I call the rescue and find that Sven is still too young and not even weaned. It is great, as we could use a few more weeks of healing time anyway. Lars can hardly contain his excitement as I pay for Sven over the phone and decide to pick him up when he is ready, shots and worming taken care of. I also add $200 to the bill as a donation, smiling as Lars kisses me.

"Arlene, I can't wait! You are too good." We hear the delight of the donation surprise from the woman on the phone, and she promises that she will email us with progress updates and pictures of Sven. We thank her, and Lars wants to go shopping right away for a crate, collar, toys, and a nice bed. Corralling his excitement, I tell him that we can go to PetSmart tomorrow after our appointment at the VA. He reluctantly agrees and we talk about the changes we will need to make in the house, a doggie door for starters and per-haps replacing the carpet in the living room with hardwood floor.

"Once you have your prosthesis, you will not need the wheelchair so much around the house." He winces, and I assure him that he will not need to worry because we will find the right fit and make it comfortable for him to wear.

"I hope so. I won't wear it if it hurts too much."

I kiss him and he relaxes a bit. We spend a quiet week at home and watch as a craftsman cuts a door in a wall and provides outside access for Sven. Lars is getting more excited as the time nears to meet our husky puppy.

CHAPTER SIX

We drive to the VA for a progress appointment with Dr. Todd. Lars is apprehensive and sweat beads on his forehead as we pull into the parking lot. I pat his knee and tell him, "You will do great; just relax." Dr. Todd comes into the room and begins his exam of Lars. Pleased with the appearance, he pushes and pulls the stump, watching for any reaction from Lars. No pain. He produces two prostheses from a cabinet, and Lars is immediately anxious. Dr. Todd reassures him this is only the start of finding the right leg for him and explains that the length must be perfect so there is no difference in his gait or height.

"We have estimated the correct length for you, and I want to put this on you and see if you can stand with full weight on the stump. Lars, pay attention so when we find the right one, you can easily put it on."

Lars watches Dr. Todd and tells him he is nervous. With a prosthetic strapped onto Lars's remaining limb, Dr. Todd tells him to slowly stand and put his weight on the right leg. Lars gingerly stands, and we watch for signs of pain. "Can I take a step or two?"

"Yes, but slowly. Tell me how it feels and if there's any pain or pressure."

"No pain, a little pressure on the inside left." Then he looks over at me, a questioning look on his face. "Arlene, why are you crying?"

"Oh Lars, you are going to be fine. I'm just not sure if I want to give up so much care of you." He smiles at me before he turns back to the doctor. "Can I walk a little more, Dr. Todd?"

"Yes Lars, walk to the end of the room and walk back." Lars does and shows a little unbalance as he turns to walk back, so Dr. Todd says, "Show me exactly where you feel pressure and tell me how you feel having a substitute leg." Lars shows Dr. Todd the spot where pressure exists and tells him, "This is so weird. I never thought I would like an artificial leg."

"Well, Lars, we still have a way to go, but I'm very pleased at this stage." He unlocks it and slowly releases the straps, noting any red marks left behind on the stump. "Okay, Lars, I want to see you in six weeks for further evaluation and fittings. Your stump is still healing, and you need to continue your strength exercises. Call me if you have pain or need a question answered. Arlene, we miss you, but you are the best thing for Lars."

Lars squeezes my hand and leans over to kiss me. "She is the best, for sure." I give Lars his crutch, and he turns and asks to wear the leg home. "Soon Lars, soon." He cannot contain his enthusiasm on the way home. "Baby, you were right. I'm going to be a whole man again except for this," he says, holding up the stump of his left arm. "I never want to get a claw hand for this—I can't imagine touching you with a cold metal claw."

"I agree, Lars, and my hand is yours whenever you need it. You know, we should celebrate tonight. Our journey has come a long way." I stop at the liquor store and choose a chilled champagne at twenty-five dollars a bottle—not the best but good enough for us. We are practical and need to watch our funds. Our trip to Norway will be in about a month, and it edges closer now that Lars will have a right leg to walk on.

We return home and drink a few glasses

of champagne. Lars is so excited as he rattles off what things he can do with a right leg. "I want to get some great jeans, so people won't know that I don't really have a full right leg. But for now, let's go celebrate in bed."

We are both ready to join our bodies and celebrate our deep love for one another. Before we get to the bed, Lars tells me, "I sweated so much at the VA that I should shower first."

"Lars, you are fine, and I want you as you are now." I pull his sweatpants off and kiss his stump, trailing kisses to his rigid cock. He pulls at my nipples as I pull at his cock. He shifts and says, "I'm close, I want to take you now."

I settle him on me, and he pounds into me, only just a few minutes, garbling my name as he climaxes. "Baby, I love you. Thank you for giving me a whole life again." Tears run down his face, and he sobs on my chest. "So many years I was lost, never to be a man again, and then you found me and loved me, even though I don't have a hand and a leg."

"I don't notice those missing parts. I am overwhelmed by the parts you do have." I kiss him deeply and roll him over on his side. I want to lie against him, my breasts to his back and my arms around his waist. "I love you,

Lars, every part of you. You are mine. I cannot think of a time when I was happier, not even the births of my three kids. They did not share such an extraordinary journey with me before they were born, so I didn't feel such powerful love for them as they were strangers, whereas you a part of me, Lars." I tell myself, *quit thinking, Arlene—you are just overwhelmed right now. Hold Lars tighter to you and go to sleep. It is been a day of wonder. Sleep, sleep.*

CHAPTER SEVEN

Six weeks go by quickly. We have replaced the floor in the living room. Now it shines and will be easy to clean and navigate with a wheelchair when needed. We have shopped for clothes and shoes for Lars as his wardrobe was very meager: one left shoe, sweats, and no jeans. Now he has new shoes, new jeans, and soft, supple underwear that will be easy for Lars to pull on with only one hand. However, I will have to help him secure his jeans and tie the laces of his shoes.

Lars has thrown himself into rehab, strengthening his leg and right arm. He has gained a few pounds, and his chest has chiseled to an incredibly attractive definition—one that I cannot resist running my hands over, frequently questing lower to another part that has not changed. We pore over the books we purchased about Norway and

Viking history. Lars points out towns, fjords, and foods of his country. I learn about the ancient gods of the Vikings and what their culture was like.

We see Dr. Todd, and he goes over the adjustments he has made to the prosthetic. I show him a pair of Nikes for Lars to try with the leg. He tells Lars to put the leg on and then loosens the straps a bit. "We don't want to cut off your circulation. Stand up, Lars, and see how it feels."

"Wait," I say. "Let me get your shoes on. Okay, you are good to go." Lars walks to the end of the room, and when he turns around, tears are running down his cheeks. He starts to sob, and I stand and pull him to my chest. He quietly murmurs, "I never dreamed this day would come." Tears pool in my eyes as well. Just seeing this strong Viking cry because he is standing on two feet is gut-wrenching, so I tell Dr. Todd to give us a few minutes. "Cry all you want, Lars, and I'll cry with you. A day never imagined but somehow here."

We hold tight to each other and Lars says, "I'm so sorry, baby; a man should not cry like this."

"Oh Lars, I love it when you do. You bare your soul, and I love you naked and brave." I wipe away his tears and call Dr. Todd back in. His eyes are wet as well, and he tells us this journey has been one of the most rewarding of his career.

Lars hugs him and says, "Arlene convinced me it would be possible, and you made it possible." Such an unusual but wonderful joining of three hearts, working as one. Dr. Todd tells Lars that it is early for release and for wearing his prosthesis, but he is confident that Lars can walk out of here. "Lars, you are ready; just don't overdo it, and Arlene, watch the stump. Here is some moleskin for the stump and call me if you need anything." I hug Dr. Todd as he opens the door for Lars and me to walk out. Knowing the risks of early release, I know that I must temper his enthusiasm. We will take it slow for a few walks around the neighborhood to find a route for Sven and Lars; then I will call and arrange to pick up Sven if our walks go well. When we return home, Lars leads me to the bedroom and takes me with all his passion. I wake so happy in the morning. We have a big breakfast, dress for a walk, and I remind Lars not to pull the straps too tight. I bend to tie the laces of his Nikes and he pulls me to the door. We walk around the block, and I ask how he feels.

"Great, Arlene, great. I want to go again."

"Okay but tell me if you have pain." We return home, and I tell Lars to take the leg off so I can look at the stump. A few light red marks but that is all. Lars pushes me to the bed and savagely kisses me. "I want you bad." I pull his sweatpants down, and he takes me violently with passion. "I'm sorry, baby, but I needed that and you." The phone rings. It is the husky rescue, and they say we can pick up Sven tomorrow. We need to get his dog food, so I rush back to the bedroom to tell Lars. He quickly puts his leg on and asks me to tie his shoes. Ready, we go to the pet store and get Sven's food. Lars is like a kid, picking up toys and a matching leather collar and leash.

The next morning, Lars wakes before me, starts the coffee, and brings me a cup. I tie his shoes, we dress warmly, and we are off to get Sven. A four-hour drive later, we are there. We go into the receiving area and Darlene, the woman we have spoken with on the phone, comes over to greet and update us. Sven is microchipped, doggie door ready and house-broken, and ready for a new life. Darlene turns to go get him and goes through a wide door opening to a large yard filled with dogs of every color. She whistles and says, "Sven!"

A small ball of fluffy white-and-silver fur runs to her and begs to be held. Lars bends down a bit awkwardly and calls for Sven to come. Like a shot, the ball of fur runs to Lars and jumps into his arms. Overcome, Lars clutches the dog tightly, kissing him and whispering something in Norwegian that I do not understand.

"Oh baby, he is wonderful. Just what I imagined." He struggles to stand, unfamiliar with bending the artificial leg and his one hand holding Sven. I help him up and he releases Sven, who runs around and goes to a large basket in the corner. He pulls a toy and begins to chew on the ear of a bedraggled teddy bear. Sven brings the toy to Lars and stretches out over his right foot. We talk with Darlene and learn Sven's feeding schedule and how to register him for a license in our county. Lars picks him up and we hug Darlene, thanking her for her rescue efforts and promising to stay in touch.

CHAPTER EIGHT

We get in the car, and Lars says that he will hold Sven for the trip back. He struggles to fasten his seat belt while holding a wiggling puppy, so I reach over and fasten the seat belt and pet Sven. I kiss Lars and we are off. Sven curls up on Lars's lap and sleeps while Lars pets him, stroking the soft fur back and forth, back and forth. I stop at a rest stop two hours later and put a leash on Sven. A few feet away from the car, Lars grabs the leash and stands, waiting for the puppy to pee. Sven pees and then, startled, jerks the leash and throws off Lars's balance enough to force him to grab a fence rail. I gather Sven and we load back into the car, resuming our drive. "Arlene, I'm sorry. I didn't expect Sven to pull so hard."

"I know; we will talk about this again at home." Sven settles onto Lars's lap and sleeps for the rest of the trip. At home, he runs around the house exploring and then goes through the doggie door. He is back five minutes later, so I get his bowls and feed him the prescribed food and water. He plays with a few toys and then flops into his new soft bed. Lars and I have a quick dinner, then I take his hand and we go to the bedroom. He knows I am not happy from the rest of the quiet trip home. I start by telling Lars that a dog requires certain attention and that he will be at risk if he walks Sven himself.

"I'm not a baby; I can handle him."

"You might be able to now, but he is a puppy, soon to be 100 to 150 pounds. Huskies are strong dogs, and you have some limitations that could prevent you from containing him. Dogs are unpredictable, and Sven could jerk you in front of a car or something. I need you to be careful and safe because you are my life." Lars is confused, and we have our first strong words.

"Lars, all I ask is that if you walk Sven, I am with you."

"Arlene, I'm a man. I can handle this."

"Lars, you have a new artificial leg, you have no left hand, and you are open to abuse out on the street. I could get you up if you fall,

I could stop a dog fight if needed, any number of things that I can do that you, perhaps, could not. I know you are a man, Lars, my love, and I will fight to keep you safe any way I can." I move to kiss him, but he says, "Just when I began to think I'm whole, you make me feel broken."

"You aren't broken, Lars; you just have a few limitations others do not have. You are all man to me, one I love more than life, so do not take that away from me. Now baby, show me how much of a man you are."

I begin to pull his sweatpants down and he brushes my hand away. "I can do it myself."

I kiss him deeply and sense his resistance. "Oh Lord, forgive me. I only want you safe and protected as much as possible. Remember, you are exposed when you are alone outside. You are not partially hidden, and you do not have a weapon or a buddy to help you. Think of me as your buddy, by your side and willing to help always."

Tears fall and Lars says, "I can't even walk my fucking dog. What kind of a man can't do that?"

"Millions, Lars. Quadriplegics, no arms like John had, and others. You have much more than others with my help as a nurse because I know some limitations you do not realize. Number one, your stump is not fully healed, you do not have a real foot on your right leg, and a prosthesis cannot sense changes in terrain. Number two, you have no left hand to give you additional strength. But you are NOT broken. Think of athletes dropping a catch, unable to press a weight or losing a race. That does not make them less of an athlete, only more vulnerable to outside influences. Now, drop this and let me make love to you before Sven wakes."

He is receptive this time, and we make passionate love. I hear Sven go through the doggie door and return a few minutes later. Lars calls him and he runs to the bedroom, but he cannot get on the bed. I reach down and pull the fuzz ball up, placing him on Lars's chest. Soon, they are both sleeping.

I get up and go make a cup of coffee and think over the last few hours. Lars still needs time to come to terms with everything, so I must watch what I say and how I speak with him. My eyes grow heavy, so I go and retrieve Sven from Lars, putting him in his bed, now located in our room. It has been a day. Time for sleep.

Sven wakes us with puppy noises, clawing

the bed to get up to us. I pick him up and carry him to the kitchen, where he drinks water before disappearing through the doggie door. Lars joins me in the kitchen, wincing a little. He fills Sven's bowl, and the puppy returns to scarf up his food. I notice Lars wince again, so I tell him that I want to check his stump. He grunts but heads to the bedroom. I remove his leg and grimace when I see the deep red marks on the end of his stump. I get a mirror so Lars can see the marks, and he frowns when he sees them.

"Lars, yesterday was the first day you had the leg on all day, and you know it is not fully healed, so you have pressure injuries. I do not want you to wear the leg today and maybe not even tomorrow. I will call Dr. Todd and tell him about the pressure injuries and see if we can get a cream to help toughen your skin."

I call Dr. Todd and he says, "Too much, too soon. Not enough time for the scar tissue to form and toughen the end. Keep it clean, do not wear the leg for a while, and put a good moisturizer on it. Let's say three days without the leg, use the moleskin, and when you do come in, we'll see if it has gotten worse."

I relate to Lars the news, clean his stump well, and apply Eucerin to the stump. We are going to spend the day in bed with Sven and watch some football. I make pancakes and bacon for breakfast; then we return to bed for a few subdued hours. He says, "You are right, baby. I should listen better."

"Yes, and you should eat your breakfast and watch the game. Call me if you want the bathroom." I do the dishes, and I am letting Sven out the door when I hear Lars call me. "I need the bathroom." I take him his crutch, and he tells me to give him some time, so I kiss him and return to the kitchen. I check what I need to make meatloaf for dinner and start a load of laundry. Lars will need sweat-pants, not jeans, for the next few days. I go to the bedroom and Lars is back in bed, resting. I turn on the TV, and I tell him that I am going to the store and that I will be back soon. I give him a kiss and pat Sven, telling him, "Be good, and I'll bring you a treat."

I rush through the store and return to my sleeping males, happy and content. I put away the groceries and throw the laundry in the dryer. Quietly, I get into bed beside my favorite guys and enjoy the heat of close contact. We sleep for several hours, and Sven wakes us up with puppy noises. I put him down and he runs for the doggie door. Leaning over to kiss Lars, I notice that he smells of dog. "You need a shower." We get to the shower, and Lars wants me to move the shower chair forward. I look at him and he smiles. Turning the water to a comfortable temperature, I soap up while he stands behind me, crutch under his arm for support.

"Bend over, baby; I want to take you." He grabs the back of the shower chair for balance, and once stable, he pushes into me and comes loudly. He starts to wobble, and I spin the chair around to him and sit him down.

"Stay still. I will wash your hair and get you back to bed. You are a project, Lars, a project." I get Lars to bed, check his stump which looks better, and put sweatpants on him and myself. Sven is at our bedside in his bed. The family sleeps away the afternoon, warm, content, and at peace.

We spend the next few days quiet at home. I pay bills, and Lars spends time with Sven. The marks on his stump have disappeared, and I have lined the end of his leg with a thick layer of moleskin. On Wednesday, I wake Lars with oatmeal, coffee and warm clothes. He puts on his leg and when standing, mentions that he feels great because the moleskin helps. We call Sven, put on his leash, and go for a short walk in through the neighborhood. I check the stump again when we get home—no marks, no swelling. I kiss it and say, "Looks good, Lars, but we need to take it slow."

He nods and says, "That was fun, and I can definitely see that Sven will be a challenge as he gets bigger. Right again, Arlene." We start to take Sven for longer walks and grow more comfortable each day. Dr. Todd is pleased and again warns us not to overdo it. It is time for our trip, so I check our tickets for Norway and make sure I have all possible medications, our passports, and our IDs. We drive to the husky rescue the day before we leave since Darlene will be taking care of Sven while we are gone. With our mail being held and our bags packed, I call the airline and request a wheelchair for Lars.

CHAPTER NINE

At the airport, it will be an exceedingly long walk to the gate, going from the domestic to the international gates. Lars will resist using the wheelchair, but he will be grateful when we get to our gate.

His mom and uncle will be meeting us at the airport. His mom has not seen Lars for over thirty years and cannot wait to see him. Will she recognize him? Yes, I think so. He is much older and a bit heavier, but still blond and handsome. She let me know in a recent conversation that she plans to cook his favorite foods and have many childhood friends over to see us while we are visiting. "We love you, Arlene, as does Lars. He has told us all about you."

Lars is overly excited about the trip but disappointed that we cannot take Sven; the quarantine time is longer than we can be there. When we drive Sven to his temporary home and it is time to leave, Lars becomes quite emotional. Sven licks his face, removing the tears, then Lars gives him a fierce hug and we are off.

We take a cab to the airport since the parking fee for our long absence will be too much. During the ride, I caress Lars's leg, and we talk about Norway, places to visit, places to see, a few lessons in Norwegian, and the krone, Norway's money. We register and check our bags, then head for the escalator to the upper floor and gate. The escalator proves to be a challenge for Lars, but I hold him steady and negotiate the moving stairs with just a few awkward movements. Seated on the first plane, it begins— our trip to Lars's ancestral home.

We land in New York and make our way to the international departure terminal. Thankful for the wheelchair I ordered for Lars, I notice the strain of travel already evident in his face. We settle in our seats; grateful the restrooms are close by. We take the proffered water, and I hand Lars a pain pill. "Take a nap and rest".

"Thanks, baby, I needed this." Oslo is eight hours away and flying at over thirty thousand feet, I know there will be little to see. Lars nods off, and I pull out the book on Norway to learn more of what awaits us.

We have a snack a few hours into the flight, refusing dinner, and then Lars needs the restroom. No crutch for support, so he clutches tightly to the seat backs to make his way back and forth. When he returns, he falls heavily into his seat, and I notice that he is sweating profusely. "Can I have another pill, baby? My leg is throbbing." Travel is difficult for us but will be worth it. Soon, Lars goes back to sleep, and I follow.

We both wake when the pilot announces the weather and time in Oslo, where we will be landing in fifteen minutes. I adjust my watch and take in the countryside through my window now that it is much more visible because of our lower altitude. We land in Oslo, thirty miles from town, and I have Lars sit down while I negotiate the difficult retrieval of our luggage. He calls his mother and tells her to wait for us outside the terminal. As we head through the doors, Lars points out his mom and uncle, who both rush over and hug Lars tightly. Tears all around, and I am surprised that they are English-speaking. His uncle, Tovar, brings the car around, and we load the luggage into the old Volvo trunk. We talk about our flight, and Lars asks about various relatives. His mom talks rapidly, occasionally shifting into Norwegian.

We have two hours before we get to the house. Lars rubs his stomach and I know he is uncomfortable, but I do not want to give him another pain pill. Another hour and he has shifted several times, so I relent and give him a pill. His mother asks what is wrong, and I explain that his leg hurts and that our long travel day has not helped. She is curious about the leg and why he does not have an artificial hand. I patiently explain the revision surgery, that it is still early in the healing process, and that Lars is just getting used to a prosthetic leg.

"Oh Lars, honey, I'm so sorry. What can I do?" Lars responds to his mom, "Don't worry—it will just take time. Hey, what did you make for dinner?"

She smiles. "I have salted beef, boiled potatoes, cheese, and I made an apple pie since you always liked it, as did Papa. You and Arlene will be upstairs in your old room. Can you handle the stairs, Lars?"

"Can't wait, Mom." We arrive, and Mom shows us the house. It has changed little over the years, somewhat modern and light, but not open concept. The outside looks like the expected rough, rustic cabin, with a large chimney dominating the outside framework. Mom starts a fire and tells Lars to show us our room. We make our way up the wooden stairs slowly, holding the handsome spruce hand-rail. In the room, Lars sits on the bed imme-diately and says, "Arlene, I need to take the leg off." I nod and pull his sweatpants to his ankles. I release the straps and know why he is in pain. The stump is red and swollen, and I remember, *too much, too soon*. I ask where the bathroom, and Lars directs me down the hall and to the left. I go use the bathroom and return with a warm, soapy washcloth and gently clean the stump. Lars winces as I do and I tell him, "No more today."

I go downstairs and tell his mom, "Lars needs to rest his leg and won't be able to come downstairs for dinner." Disappointed, she goes upstairs to see Lars and I follow. She surprises Lars, and he moves to cover his stump. She sits down on the bed and pulls the down comforter aside. "Let me see what the war did to my boy."

Lars says, "No, Mom, you don't need to see this." She ignores him and pulls the comforter aside. She stares at the stump, and Lars says, "I'm still your boy, Mom. I just don't have everything left that you gave me." She hugs Lars, wipes her eyes, and tells him that she will bring his dinner to him.

I follow his mom downstairs, hug her, and tell her that it has been a very long journey and that Lars is still not fully healed, if he ever will be. She starts to cry again and says, "The war took Sven and took so much from my other son. Their papa would cry too if he were here."

I fold my arms around her. "Lars has me to love and help him, and I have him. I love him dearly and will protect him in everything."

She kisses my cheek and goes about the kitchen to prepare a tray for Lars and me. "You go back to him and I will bring dinner up." I return to the room, and Lars is in a fetal position under the thick comforter. I kiss him and he says, "I'm so embarrassed for Mom to see the stump. I don't know what the fuck to tell her, Arlene."

"Baby, she is your mom. She brought you into this world, and then she must see her son with missing parts. She also lost your brother, and your papa died. You are the only one left and damaged by war, but do not feel guilty or embarrassed. She loves you. I love you. Now, sit up; she will be bringing dinner up."

He tells me that he needs the toilet and I frown. "I need to figure out how to get you there and back. Sit still, and I'll be right back." I rush downstairs and tell his mom the situation. She thinks for a minute and says, "Papa's walking stick. Perfect." She pulls it from a small closet by the fireplace, and I go back to Lars. He stands and tests the stick for balance. I put my arm around his waist and we slowly make our way to the bathroom. He holds tightly to the stick, and I hold his penis so he can pee. He winks at me. "Just like the old days, baby." I squeeze him and say, "Yes Lars, you continue to be my project." We make our way back to the bedroom, and I put his sweatpants back on with a smile. "Your mom has seen enough today!" We hear a soft knock and I go to open the large, ornately carved door, knowing she will have a tray in her hands, and I comment on beautiful the door is.

"Lars's papa carved this door, including the wolf proudly outlined in the center, because Lars loved wolves and dogs when he was little."

I smile at her. "He still does; let me show you some pictures after dinner."

Lars and I eat the hot meal, the beef a little too salty for my taste, but Lars loves it. His mom returns after a while and takes the dinner tray, returning to the kitchen for the strong coffee, creamer, and the apple pie she has put together to finish our meal.

I sit her down, saying, "Here are some pictures of Sven and us." She looks surprised, and Lars softly tells her, "I named him Sven." She tears up again and asks how old Sven is and if he is good, and Lars tells her all about him and where he is now. "Oh Lars, I have missed you so much. Your papa would be so proud. Sven could pull our sled!"

"No, Mama, he is too young, and he would need help to pull it."

I kiss Lars, pick up the tray, and go back downstairs with Mom, telling her to sit down and eat her dinner and I will do the dishes. No dishwasher, so I fill the sink and add some soap. Noticing a drying rack, I grab it and place it on the counter. While I work on the dishes, I tell Lars's mom that he will need to rest for a few days, but I need to get him a crutch so he can walk without his leg. She calls out in Norwegian to Lars's uncle, who has been out by the fire snoozing. He comes into the kitchen and she continues in

Norwegian, asks if he can get a crutch for Lars and explains why it is needed. He tells her that there is a secondhand shop close by that has several them. She turns to me and explains what she asked and says that we can get a crutch in the morning. I thank them both and tell them good night because it has been a long day. Mom says to wake her if we need anything and that she will bring breakfast to us in the morning. I hug her and say, "Thank you; your boy is home and happy."

We had planned to spend a few days touring Oslo, Lars wanting to see the many changes made over the years. Instead, we will spend the days here and allow the stump to heal a bit. I go to the bathroom and fill the white mug sitting on a shelf with water. Lars needs a pill and a good rest. I kiss him and tuck him in, warm beneath the down feather quilts so commonly used by Scandinavians on their beds. He rolls to watch me undress, then pulls me to his side.

"I love you, Arlene. I don't think I can do anything tonight, sorry."

I snuggle up to him, my breasts against his back and my arm around his waist. "Don't you worry about that. I will spoon with you, and you can sleep. Wake me if you need the bathroom."

He is already asleep, so I squeeze his waist and close my eyes.

CHAPTER TEN

We both sleep well until Mom knocks on the door. It is a little cold in the room as she bustles in with hot coffee and apple turnovers warm from the oven. She leans over and whispers to Lars, "Your uncle has a crutch for you." He looks over to me, and I explain that his stump needs to rest for a few days before he uses the leg. His mom calls his uncle to bring up the crutch, and he brings it over to the bed. Lars thanks him in native tongue, and his uncle nods his head and heads downstairs. Lars says that he needs to use the bathroom, so I take the crutch and hold it for him to support himself. It is too short, so I quickly adjust the height, and we walk slowly down the hall. I hold his penis again as he relieves himself, and I tell him to sit and try to poop. He gives me a look and says, "Okay, Mommy." I head back to the bedroom and fluff the comforters and change into warmer clothes. Looking out the window, I see it is snowing, and several inches have covered the evergreens in the large yard. I go back down the hall and check on Lars. He is standing over the sink washing his face and asks for his toothbrush. "Sure, I'll be right back."

When I return, he is sitting on the toilet, eyeing the shower. "Do you think I could shower there?"

"No, Lars, no chairs and no grip bars—too dangerous." I tell him Mom wants us downstairs because she has company coming. He frowns, and I tell him that I will help him down the stairs. We head back to the bedroom and I explain how we can get down the stairs safely. He grunts and we start to head down, slowly taking it step by step with my arm around his waist. He is sweating when we are finally at the bottom. I settle him on a comfortable chair in the living room. The fire is crackling, and the room smells of burning wood—a smell that I love. His mother brings a cup of coffee to him, and I go to get him some water as well because he needs fluids. His mom tells him in Norwegian who is coming, and he smiles: his old teenage girlfriend, an aunt, and a few childhood friends. She will have haddock, potatoes, and fresh melon for lunch. Lars says, "Mom, don't do too much. Let Arlene help you."

I kiss him and go into the kitchen with his mom. We finish the dishes, and I tell her, "Mom, I think it's easier if Lars and I stay in a nearby hotel. He needs a large shower and no stairs until the leg is better." She understands and reels off the names of a few hotels. I tell her what we will need, and she says that she will call and make a reservation for tonight. I thank her and return to Lars to explain the change in plans, and he agrees, knowing that it is too hard for him here. His mother comes to us later and tells us that she has made reservations at Scandic Holmenkollen Park. Lars turns to me and tells me that the hotel has views of the Holmenkollen Ski Jump. He asks his mom how much it is, and she tells us 1,500 kroner, which is expensive, but the hotel has everything we need. Forty minutes north of us in a wooded forest area, we should be comfortable. He asks his mom if his uncle can drive us, and she tells him that she already asked Tovar, and he will be happy to help. A bell rings at the door, and several blond, blue-eyed women and men come into the living room. One woman advances to Lars and kisses his cheek. She speaks Norwegian to him and pats his leg. I find out later that she was his teenage girlfriend. The conversation flows in the native tongue, and I realize how guttural the words are. Lars is animated and occasionally turns to me to relay in English what they are talking about. Mom comes in and announces lunch, so his former girlfriend and I returned to the kitchen to help serve. Lars asks for my phone and passes it around, showing Sven to the small group. Lunch is delicious, haddock cooked perfectly, though no tartar sauce—I am just too American. Mom also brings a bottle of aquavit, a dill-flavored spirit commonly served with fish. Lars says he has not had any for thirty years, and the conversations become livelier as the bottle empties. He whispers to me that he needs the bathroom.

"Do we have to go upstairs?" I ask.

"No, Mom has one in her room." He guides me through a maze of rooms off the living room and stops at another beautifully carved door. "Papa loved to carve edelweiss, which is Mom's favorite flower."

The bathroom is large and bright and has a soft sheepskin rug down the center of it. I pull the rug aside, and Lars moves to the toilet. After he is done, I flush the toilet and bend to replace the rug before we leave. In his mom's room, Lars shows me several photos of the family in earlier years. I note the catch in his voice as he points out Sven, who looked so much like Lars with his large blue eyes, though Sven's hair had been darker. He then pulls an ornately framed picture of his dad from the wall. "My papa." Tears pool in his eyes as he softly whispers, "Home." I pull him tightly to me, and we just stand together for a moment or two.

"It is a lovely family, Lars. I'm sorry it took so long to get you back here."

We return to the living room as the group is putting on coats and furs to help us get ready to go. Mom drains a glass of aquavit and tells Lars that his uncle will be here in fifteen minutes, so I jump up and go upstairs to pack. I am unable to fit the leg into a suitcase, so I decide I will just carry it. I place the suitcase in the hall and go downstairs with Lars, his leg under my arm. I set the leg down on a side table and then bring the suitcases down beside it. He hugs his mom hard, kisses her, and says something in Norwegian. She smiles, kisses him, and says to call tomorrow. We say goodbye and she hugs me. "Arlene, I'm so happy my boy found you. Take care of him."

I hug her hard and tell her, "No worries. I will always take care of Lars. He is my life." His uncle Tovar comes in carrying a snow shovel and puts the bags in the car. The sidewalk has been cleared of snow, but ice remains, so we very carefully walk to the car. One more hug for Mom, and we are off to the hotel.

Lars and his uncle speak Norwegian back and forth during the forty-minute drive. There is a lot of snow, and it is noticeably colder as we get closer to the hotel. Lars says Holmenkollen is just beyond the hotel, hidden by snow. I hope to see it over the next few days. Thousands of lights shine below us in the ancient city of Oslo. As we pull up, the facade of the hotel resembles one of Norway's rustic churches, with the entry a picture post-card of Norway. Lars and I tell Tovar thank you and goodbye and to be careful driving home. A bellhop loads our luggage, and I pull the leg from the cart. We are on the ground floor so luckily, it is just a short distance to our room. Once inside, I check the bathroom for grab bars and to assess the size of the shower. Lars flops down on the bed. The room is good, rustic, but it has everything we need. I shut the door and return to Lars, who suggests that we shower. I nod yes, but since there is no shower chair, it will have to be quick. I get us naked, turn on the shower, and get out our bodywash as the hotel soap seems rough and has a medicinal odor. To make it easier, I put the bathmat on the shower floor, and Lars steps onto it, his crutch tight under his arm. I soap both of us and wash our hair, adjusting the shower head to rinse us off. I exit to quickly grab some dry towels; then I lead Lars over to the bed, pulling back the down comforter to tuck him in and warm up. I dry his hair and mine, then bend carefully to look at his stump. It is still red and swollen. I give Lars a soft kiss and travel my hand down his body. Lars does the same with me, and we make gentle love, the snow falling outside of the large windows. I hold him to me for a few moments, then get up to bring him a glass of water and two Tylenol. I know he has not had a bowel movement for three days, and the codeine pain pills will not help. It would be difficult to deal with the constipation during our trip, so I take the steps to stop it while Lars sleeps peacefully.

CHAPTER ELEVEN

We wake early. There is a small restaurant in the hotel, so I decide to order room service: ham and eggs, coffee and Norwegian sourdough toast. I get Lars up and dressed, then have him go in and sit on the toilet. He smiles, knowing what is expected. He comes out of the bathroom shortly after, shaking his head as the bell outside our door announces our breakfast arrival. I notice Lars shaking his head when I go to tip the waiter, and after he smiles and leaves, Lars explains that it is not necessary to tip in Norway.

I hand him a few pills to help with the constipation and he says, "I hope these work—I am already binding up."

"I hope so, too; I will have to take you to a hospital if you become impacted." He frowns, and I change the subject.

"Come, let's sit down and watch the snow."

We sit in the rather stiff Danish-style chairs facing the window, and we can just barely make out the top of the ski jump. Lars tells me about how the jump is used in the Olympics and World Ski Jumping Championships. It is enormous, and I wish we could go see it, but Lars is too fragile at the moment. We look out the window for an hour as the snow continues, and then Lars says, "Let's go back to bed."

I say, "Great," and we return to the soft, warm bed. I reach for him, pull down his sweatpants, and take him in my mouth, drawing him in and out, in and out. He is panting and breathes, "Take me, baby—I want to come in your mouth," so I suck harder, and he groans as he releases.

I kiss him, and he asks, "How can you stand the taste of my semen?"

I tell him, "Yeah, it doesn't taste very good, but the feelings I have for you cancel the bad taste. I love watching you pant and shiver, closing your eyes when you come. I love you, Lars. You should sleep; I'm going to have a bath and shave my legs."

"Okay, but maybe I should join you?"

"No, I would have trouble getting you in

and out. You sleep, and I'll join you soon." I grab some clothes, my razor, and a few toiletries, and go into the bathroom to fill the tub. I squirt bodywash under the faucet, and fragrant suds begin to bubble under the strong water pressure. I slide into the tub, lean back, and enjoy the hot water as I wait for the hair of my legs to soften. I shave my underarms and my legs, then drain the tub and step out. Refreshed, dry, and dressed warmly, I get into bed and pull back the comforter, enjoying the sight of my sleeping Lars. Cozy and content, I close my eyes and fall asleep beside the man I love.

We sleep away the day and wake at dinnertime, snow still falling outside. I order room service for us: cod, rice, and fresh vegetables. His mom calls and they talk in Norwegian. She tells Lars that they would come to visit tomorrow, but there is too much snow for the drive north. He tells her that he understands and to play it safe and stay home. Our dinner arrives just in time, as we are both hungry.

Later, after our meal, Lars says that his stomach hurts. I run my hands over his belly and tell him he is constipated but not impacted. "We will see how you are tomorrow."

He motions me to the bed. As we lie

down, he runs his hands over my smooth legs, works his way down to my sex, playing with me briefly. "I'm sorry, baby. I just don't feel very well."

"Oh Lars, just relax. We don't have to."

"I don't understand why this happens to me," he mumbles.

I explain that the codeine pills cause it, and some people have tendencies for this, noting that he unfortunately does. "We will see how you are in the morning, and if you still can't go, I'll put some strong suppositories in you."

"You have some with you?"

"Yes, Lars. Luckily, as a nurse, I know what I might need for you."

He groans. "I'm sorry, baby, to always need you so much."

Trying to convince him not to worry, I get up and push the room service cart out into the hall. I pull some massage oil from my bag, get a towel and return to Lars. I pull up his sweatshirt and tell him to roll over so that I can give him a massage. I knead his shoulders and work my way down his back. Pulling his sweatpants down a bit, I make my way to his ass and the tops of his thighs. I bring my hands up and spread oil over his anus. Feeling

Lars grow tense, I return to move my hands along his back. "Relax, Lars, no suppositories until tomorrow, if you need it."

"It's just so private, baby. It bothers me."

I turn him over, kiss him deeply, and tell him, "Lars, I know every inch of you, and I love every inch of you. Do not ever feel ashamed or embarrassed. You are my mate for life, despite any complications."

He kisses me and whispers, "Arlene, will you marry me?"

"We are already married; we just don't have a paper to prove it."

He persists, asking, "What if something happens to me or to you? You wouldn't be able to make Medicare decisions for me at the VA, and if something happens to you, I wouldn't be able to say anything either."

I look into his eyes for a long moment. "You are right, Lars. When we get back home, we can get married. I love you so much, even though you are a pain in the ass." I smack his backside with a laugh, then follow it up with a kiss.

As he drifts off to sleep, I close my eyes and think about what he told me. He is of course right—I had not even thought about it. *We really should marry. And see a lawyer about our assets and draw up wills. Or per-haps set up a trust account so that it is in place before something happens, God forbid. For now, sleep. We can talk about this again, maybe on the flight home.*

CHAPTER TWELVE

We wake to light streaming through the tall windows: sunshine, the first in days. Lars heads to the bathroom to sit on the toilet, and I go out, bringing back coffee and Dutch apple pastries for 200 kroner. Pretty expensive breakfast. Lars is in bed when I return. He looks at me with a grim face. "No luck. Let's get it over with, and then we can have breakfast."

I set everything down and go to get the suppositories and some lubricant. I have Lars lie on his side while I put lubricant on my index finger. Spreading his butt cheek, I slowly insert both capsules in his ass. I lightly kiss both cheeks, pat him, and tell him to roll over. "All done, my love. These may work very quickly, so tell me as soon as you feel an urge." I go to the bathroom and wash my hands thoroughly. We have our coffee and apple pastries and then sit on the bed, waiting for the magic to happen. Fifteen minutes later, Lars yelps, "Fuck, I need to go! I don't think I can get to the toilet!"

Shit, what to do? I grab a towel and the bedside trash can and put it behind his ass, keeping the towel handy.

"Fuck, I hate this!"

"Not exactly my favorite thing either, Lars. Remember this next time you want a pain pill." I catch everything in the trash can and towel. It goes on for several minutes, and finally he says, "I think that's it."

I tell him to hold the can against his ass, and I run to get a washcloth to clean him up. Back with a wet soapy washcloth, I pull the trash can away and clean him up. Then I take the trash can and dump the contents in the toilet, pour some bath wash into the can, and fill it from the bath faucet. I leave it sitting in the tub and soap up another washcloth and towel. I return to Lars, clean him thoroughly, dry him, pull up his sweatpants, and ask him if he still wants to marry me.

"Fuck yes, Arlene; who else would put up with my literal shit?"

I laugh hard and kiss him. "I love you, Lars." I finish cleaning everything up and return to Lars. I pull his sweatpants down as he rolls his eyes.

"Christ, now what?" I tell him to calm down and that I just want to see how his stump is. I look it over carefully, and thinking it looks much better, I tell Lars one more day and we can continue our trip. I want him to rest today and keep his stump elevated, so I pile pillows under his leg and get him comfortable. Just as I join him on the bed, he apologizes, stating that he needs the toilet. I get him up and he pushes himself quickly to the bathroom. He needs to pee, and after everything that just happened, I tell him to sit down and push his penis down to pee.

"God, how do you put up with me?"

"I have infinite patience, though you require all of it," I smile.

He laughs. "What a pair we are!"

"Yes indeed, Lars, we are a pair."

Afterward, we settle into bed and I reset the pillows under his stump. "Take a nap. I'm going to get more coffee." While Lars sleeps the afternoon away, I pick up a book and read. In the evening, I go down to the restaurant and bring back bowls of chicken soup and fresh bread, and we have our dinner, looking out at the lights on the ski jump.

"Lars, we need to decide what we are going to do."

"I know," he says. "Travel doesn't agree very well with me. If you don't mind, we should spend a day with Mom and head home."

"Yes, travel is hard on me too. I'll call the airline and see if I can change our return tickets."

Lars calls his mom and speaks with her in Norwegian, telling her that we will come for a final visit tomorrow, but she tells him that she will come to us as it will be easier. I explain our situation to the airline and thankfully, they can change our tickets, though there are a few costs to do so, and it will be a two-day wait before our new flight. Grateful that we can head back home early, we are both relieved.

His mom comes the next day, and we enjoy brunch and a long visit. She is sad that we must leave, and I tell her we will pay for a ticket to the US for a visit next year. She is happy and thrilled when Lars tells her we will marry later this year. We hug and kiss, Lars tearing up when Mom says, "Don't make me wait another thirty years; I'll be dead."

We have a quiet evening in our room;

then Lars grabs my hand. "Let's go to bed. I want to make love to you." We settle in beneath the down, and he pulls my right nipple to his mouth and rolls it around with his tongue. He sinks lower, kissing my belly and running his hands to my backside. I feel his erection pressing against me, and he reaches down with his right hand and forces himself into me. We thrust against each other, the friction firing our arousal, and we come together. "Oh baby," Lars whispers, "I just could not love you more. I want to try the leg tomorrow, and maybe get outside a little bit."

"Maybe," I agree. "That would be nice." We sleep cocooned against each other, waking to another sunny day. I go down to the desk and find out that there is a shuttle twice a day to and from the ski jump. I tell Lars that we will be able to go to the jump in an hour and stay for several hours before the shuttle brings us back to the hotel.

"Let's get your leg on and see how you feel." I check the padding, telling Lars, "When you are just standing today, shift your weight off the right leg and stand on the left. It will give the stump a breather as it is just not strong enough yet."

"Okay, Dr. Arlene, I'll do it."

I smack his backside and make sure he is warmly dressed, gloves, and hat on his golden curls. We are at the meeting bench ten minutes before the shuttle, and I browse through a brochure detailing some upcoming events at the jump while Lars tells me a few names of famous Norwegian ski jumpers. We get into the shuttle and enjoy the ten-minute ride to the jump. Once there, we walk to a nearby bench and watch a class of Nordic youth training to learn ski jumping. They amuse us with their antics down the small ice hills built for them to practice on, and we wonder whether one of them could be an Olympic record holder in training. Lars says, "I always wanted to do that. Guess like a lot of things, I never will." We go into the small, rustic restaurant and sit by a window, watching jumpers edge over to the takeoff ramp and hop on it, then speed down the icy hill. Lars explains the process and describes a perfect telemark landing as we drink our hot cocoa. A few hours later, the shuttle picks us up and we return to the hotel. Housekeeping has replaced the linens and provided fresh towels, and Lars suggests that we go down to the restaurant for dinner. We clean up a bit and hold hands as we enter the dining room. Lars orders for us in

Norwegian and I am enthralled, listening to him and his charming accent. We have shrimp and a creamy fish chowder, followed by fruit and ice cream. We are drinking a local beer—dark, flavorful, and above the level of normal alcohol content. We enjoy our meal, and Lars picks the bill up from the table. "Fuck, Arlene, this place is really expensive!" he blurts out.

We go back up to our room, and Lars wants a shower. He takes his leg off and I look it over the stump—back to normal. I get into the shower with Lars and he wobbles a bit, reaching over to squeeze my shoulder. The hot water carries a faint scent of forest and suds up quickly. We hold each other and run our slippery hands up and down one another's bodies, each of us so familiar with the other's dips and curves. I turn the water off and dry us both. Returning to the bed, I pull back the comforter, and Lars pulls me to stand in front of him. "I want to take you here. Bend over, baby."

I bend to the bed, and Lars eases his cock into me. He grabs my hips for support, and I awkwardly put my hands behind me to pull him tighter, feeling his pubic hair against my backside. Lars trails his hand to my sex, rubbing furiously, then he collapses on my back as climax overcomes him. Wobbling, he yells for me to pull him onto the bed before he falls. I turn and grab his hips, pulling him to the bed and on top of me. He kisses me hard and says, "I'm not the best lover, baby."

"Oh, I disagree," I say and kiss him. "I happen to think you're the best. And I would have no other." He tells me that he wants me again, this time on top. I reach down and feel his flaccid cock. "We may need a little time, Lars."

"Help me, baby; I want you now." I roll over and take him in my mouth, tasting salt, soap, and the unique scent of a man recently satisfied. He puts his hand on my head and I feel his left stump on the other side. He presses hard on my head, forcing me to take him deeper. Panting heavily, Lars shouts out, "Bite me! Bite me!" I clamp down on him and drive him out, trailing my teeth down his length. "Baby, baby! This feels so good, I don't want to come, but I can't help it!" He explodes in me and collapses again. "God, that was good, Arlene! I love you so much, baby."

CHAPTER THIRTEEN

Dead to the world, we sleep for ten hours and wake to the sun. Our last day in Norway. I go down and bring back a light breakfast and coffee for us. I pull out our clothes for tomorrow and transfer all our laundry to the bigger suitcase, as the hotel does not offer laundry service. After making sure that we have our passports and IDs, I arrange with the front desk for a courtesy ride to the airport in the morning. We spend the afternoon with a book on sites in Norway. Lars lapses into Norwegian, and I again enjoy listening to my still-fragile Viking. I will miss seeing this unique country with its proud and ancient history, still visible to visitors. Lars senses my melancholy and hugs me. "Sorry I messed this trip up for you."

I turn to him. "Lars, you are more important to me than anything else. I could not imagine anything better than you beside me." I pull him to me, and we spend the late afternoon wrapped around each other. Lars asks me if I am less interested in him today, and I explain, "Lars, it has nothing to do with you. I am seventy years old, and my body is changing, as is my ability to have an orgasm. It takes me too long to climax, and I need your hand down there to bring me up."

"I'm sorry, baby. I didn't know—can I try right now?" I open my legs and invite him to exercise his right hand. "Talk to me; tell me what you need." I reach down and guide his hand to my clitoris. I press hard on him, and he realizes he needs to be more aggressive with me. I am panting and know I am close. He shifts to take me, and I whisper, "No Lars, you need to continue with your hand for me to come." He returns to his aggressive attention, and soon I climax. Lars follows seconds later as he ejaculates on my belly.

He sighs. "I promise to pay better attention to you. To know the mechanics needed by older women."

I turn to him. "There will come a day when you won't be able to get hard when you want to; it's just a natural sign of aging."

"I don't know, baby—you make me hard

just looking at you, thank the Lord. I hope we will still have sex in our eighties! I guess we are old, but I don't feel that with you because you make me feel young."

I roll over to him. "Well, then, how about you make me feel like a teenager again?" Lars runs his hand down my belly, trailing through some of his semen, and continues down to receive my passion. Fulfilled after our afternoon exercise session, we are both ready for a shower and a good meal. After dinner, we go back to bed and sleep until the alarm wakes us.

Packed and ready to go, we head to the front desk and settle our bill—just over 6,000 kroner, a staggering sum that upsets Lars. "I not only cost us our trip, I cost us a lot of money."

I kiss him and say, "Hush, you are worth every krone and more." It is a forty-five-minute trip to the Oslo airport, as traffic is heavy. The courtesy car drops us at the international terminal, and an agent comes over to check us in and take our luggage. It is over an hour before we get out of security and get to our gate. Lars sits down hard as I scan the tracking screens to double-check our flight time; we have just under two hours before the flight is called. Lars heads to the restroom and I go to a little café, bringing back coffee and pastries for a late breakfast. Twenty minutes later, I look at my watch as Lars has not returned from the restroom. I walk down to the restroom and ask a passing gentleman if he speaks English. He does, so I ask him to please check on Lars, as he has a few disabilities. He returns a moment later and tells me to come with him; there is only Lars in the restroom. I follow him and find Lars on the floor bleeding from his left arm, the one without a hand. I ask the stranger to notify the gate that we need some medical help. He excuses himself quickly, agreeing to get us some help. Five minutes go by, and I know that Lars is having his first PTSD attack in months, so I cradle him to me and wait for help. A medic rushes in, the red-cross symbol known all around the world blazing on his shirt and case. He asks us what happened, and I explain that Lars is a disabled vet and has PTSD attacks when he sees blood. The medic understands, and he cleans the lacerations on the stump and bandages the arm to block the sight of blood. Lars begins to come to and slowly tells us what happened.

"The floor was wet in the stall and I lost

my balance. I tried to stop the fall with my left arm, but without a hand, I went down hard. My arm was bleeding, and I couldn't move." He looks up at me in wonder. "Baby, how did you find me?" I explain as the medic and I get Lars up and stable. The medic also walks back to the gate with us, telling us goodbye and to have a safe flight. I thank him, and Lars nods.

I gather his head to my chest, not caring if it draws stares from the many passengers around us waiting for the flight. I rock him gently, telling him that this attack was not bad as I think to myself of how expensive the cost of freedom can be for a vet. *The military budget couldn't possibly cover all costs*; I grimace as I think about how all political budgets have to work with deficits.

Lars raises his head. "Saved by you again, baby. This is really becoming a habit." I kiss him, and they allow us to preboard and settle in our seats. The last-minute change has moved us from close proximity to the restrooms, but we can deal with it; we just have to get home safe. With a little over eight hours before we land in New York, we order a simple lunch of tomato soup and turkey sandwiches, water and ginger ale. I hand Lars two Tylenol, and he relaxes in his seat. Soon he is dozing beside me, and I observe that the bandage is still blood free. I also notice that Lars needs a shave, and I wonder if I should encourage him to grow a beard, a staple for the cold-weather Viking. Lars wakes a few hours from New York, needing the restroom, so I stand and head up the aisle with him. The plane hits some light turbulence and forces us to grab the seat backs. A flight attendant notices us and offers to help support an unstable Lars. We reach the restroom and Lars pushes me away. "Arlene, I can handle this; let me be." "Well, hold on to something in there, Lars, and I'll wait for you and help you get back to our seats." The turbulence continues, but we manage to get back to our seats without incident. Walking on eggshells—life with Lars.

We land in New York, negotiate customs, and wait for our flight home. I make Lars sit because I do not want him on his leg any longer than necessary. Our final flight home is relaxing, though we end up waiting two hours for our luggage. We are so ready to be home. When we finally have our luggage, I call a cab to deliver us home, to our place of solace and a welcome bed.

Inside the house, I turn the heat up, get

some water, and take two more Tylenol to Lars. We don't have dinner—we just fall into bed and sleep in peace. Lars wakes at four and asks for his crutch—time for the bathroom. I retrieve it from the closet, helping Lars make his way to the bathroom. I hold his penis for him as he goes, thinking, *Welcome home.*

CHAPTER FOURTEEN

I want Lars to rest today while I go get our mail, grocery shop, and do laundry. "Will you call Darlene so we can pick up Sven?" Lars asks.

"I want you to rest today and tomorrow; we can go get Sven on Tuesday."

Lars frowns. "I miss him."

"Yes, I do too, but he will be so excited to see you, and I want you stable."

I make meatloaf, scalloped potatoes and asparagus, and open a bottle of wine for dinner. We eat, run through the bills, and fold laundry, domestic chores so much easier at home. *Such a comfort to have our own home, money in the bank and a loving mate. So sorry not everyone can enjoy the same benefits.* We sleep well, no sex—no energy! Perhaps tomorrow.

Refreshed the next morning, we enjoy

a lazy breakfast and Lars asks, "How do you want to get married? A big wedding here? Or maybe at your daughter's?"

"Oh, something simple here, no wedding dress, maybe invite Dr. Todd and a few others." I look over to see Lars pull a box from his pocket.

"Marry me, Arlene; we need each other."

"Yes Lars, we do, intensely." The ring is quite beautiful. Diamonds and sapphires, his grandmother's legacy to her blond grandson.

"Mom gave me this the first day we were there; she knew you were the one for me."

"Oh Lars, what other woman in the world could love you like I do? You are such a project!"

I get us each a glass of white wine and sit down to call my kids. "Mom is getting married!" "Yes, we are home." "Yes, short trip. We had a few complications." "We definitely are getting married." "Yes, we are old, but we need each other, and marriage will give us some protections we wouldn't have being single." All three of my kids are pleased, and on the call with my daughter, Freyja wants to talk to Lars.

"See? I knew you were my Grandpa Lars! Please come and see me soon."

Lars tears up. "Yes, you are my grand-daughter, little one, and I love you."

"Get married in our backyard, Grandpa Lars! We will keep Yoshi in the house." Lars laughs and gives me back the phone.

"We will let you know when we know. Take care; we love you." I put the phone down and ask Lars, "So? Do you still want to marry me? If so, when and where?"

He laughs and kisses me. "Freyja wants us to get married in her backyard; she says they will leave Yoshi in the house." We decide that we will think about our plans after we pick up Sven.

Up early again the next morning, we stop at Starbucks for vanilla lattes and head to the rescue center. "Do you think we could take Sven to California if we decide to go there for the wedding?"

"I'm sure we can; I will call to find out what we need to do. Darlene probably knows what is required to fly an animal." Darlene greets us when we arrive at the rescue center and she calls for Sven, who runs straight over to Lars, licking his face in happiness. Lars squeezes the furball, who has grown a thicker coat, taking on his husky appearance. Our dog is so beautiful; he will serve as a wonderful companion to us for years to come. I tell Darlene that Lars and I are thinking about getting married in California, and we want to bring Sven with us. She tells us what we need to do regarding flights, then she says, "You know, really, California is only twelve or thirteen hours away; you should just drive." *Of course. We haven't even thought of that; another problem solved. Strange how a problem solves itself just by a suggestion of a solution. Wish I could solve all our problems that way. I think we are getting closer to the freedom Lars needs, though; he's definitely paid in spades. Perhaps with his future settled, we can live life without more reminders.* As we load Sven into the car, Darlene says, "Have a safe trip home. We enjoyed having Sven here; everyone loves that little guy." Waving as we drive away, I glance over and smile at the sight of Sven tightly curled in Lars's lap as he strokes Sven's silver fur, both relaxed and happy. Our family is back together again and soon to be officially recognized as one.

The next few weeks are busy for us as we have decided that we will marry in California. My daughter has taken on a lot of the wedding planning details, covering food, flowers, the priest, and watching the budget. I have little to do, so I order a sea-blue Mandarin-style velvet outfit, the blue the color of both Lars's and Sven's eyes.

I call Dr. Todd so he can check Lars's stump and make any recommendations based on our recent trip. Lars is less than thrilled, asking, "Do I really have to go?"

I tell him, "Remember our trip? Dr. Todd needs to see how the stump has progressed."

"Okay, I'll go to keep you happy."

I smile, knowing Lars will never understand how much Dr. Todd's surgical skills contributed to his healing. Two legs to stand on and the diminished feeling of not being a man. *Thank you so much, Dr. Todd; you are a prophet of healing.*

My wedding outfit arrives, so I unbox it and hold it up to Lars, happily confirming that the velvet matches his eyes as perfectly as I'd hoped. We go shopping and find a white shirt for Lars and some soft, suede shoes that fit his foot and prosthetic equally well, gripping the sides with proper pressure. We also decide to get a few more pairs of jeans for Lars, and he calls me to approve or turn down his choices. I see him bare-chested and draw in a breath, staring at his abdominal muscles and the defined lines that end just above his pubic hair. *Could there be anything sexier a man can show? Not for me.*

We check in with my daughter about the wedding planning and hear the girls in the background, shouting their enthusiasm for a backyard wedding. Lots of flowers and the big gazebo to shelter Grandma and Grandpa. Too old to be a giddy bride, but I do look forward to locking Lars to me and paying my share of the bridal purse.

Packed and ready, Lars, Sven, and I share a last night in our bed. Soon, Sven is told to get in his own bed, as "Daddy wants to pet Mommy." Lars snakes his hand down my body and plays a lively tune, my keys softly vibrating to his sonata.

"Take me, Lars. Join your bride-to-be with your body of treasures."

"Treasures? Arlene, we need to get you new glasses—some without fog lenses." "No Lars, I see you, all of you, and I treasure every inch, including your white ass, open to only me."

Lars covers me with his body, heat immediately producing sweat. We slide against each other with desire and passion, lying motionless afterward, sweaty limbs all entangled. Soon enough, Sven is pawing at the side of the bed, wanting to protect Lars from the danger of this woman upsetting his dad. We bring him up onto the bed and we all settle in, Sven delighted to be on Lars's chest and open to the feeling of strong fingers stroking his soft belly fur.

CHAPTER FIFTEEN

The next morning, we load up the car, making sure we have food, treats, and water for all of us. I will drive straight through, and since Lars does not drive, he can keep me awake and watchful of the road. Stopping for lunch outside of Salt Lake City, we all take a bathroom break and sit on one of the benches for a lunch of sandwiches and coffee. Sven gets a bowl of wet food, a special treat for the growing puppy.

While we eat, Lars and I discuss our upcoming visit with lawyers to set up a trust. He has a large bank account and talks about his desires to help Mom in Norway, as well as Freyja, Eliza, and me. Hopeful that the funds will outlast us, he notes that he wants to be cremated, his ashes joined with mine if possible. We fill up with gas, the tank eaten by the miles. I check the tires and water, and we continue down the eighty-mile-per-hour highway.

A long day's drive later, I call my daughter to let her know that we are just outside of town and that "Grandma and Grandpa will be hungry." We get to her house and I hear Yoshi barking when I blow the horn to announce our arrival. Sven is anxious to meet his cousin breed: a Japanese import with the traits of a fox. Both ancient breeds; I know they will be great friends. Cathryn, Sean, and the girls all come out to collect luggage and hugs and kisses. "Grandpa Lars, I love you!" Freyja exclaims as she runs over to him. Ever curious, she wants to see Lars's new leg. Cathryn restrains her while we all notice that the dogs are already friends, Yoshi trying to escape the puppy chewing his ear. We head into the house, Lars to the bathroom and me to the kitchen. Dinner smells wonderful, carefully prepared by the gourmet chefs. I opt for coffee, a bit confused by the complicated machine they use, though eventually I figure it out. Lars joins us in the kitchen and asks for coffee as well. We all sit in the living room, talking about our trip to Norway and the problems encountered. Freya comes in with Sven and Yoshi, who continue to play in front of us. "Sven is a great dog. NOW can I see your new leg?"

Lars laughs and says, "Come here, little one." He rolls up the leg of his jeans, exposing the new metal substitute for warm flesh. Freyja asks if she can touch it, and Lars nods. She runs her fingers over the cold metal, looking closely at the knee joint. Lars explains how the knee works and stands so she can see it shift and move as he flexes. Fascinated by the mechanics, she hugs Lars and says, "I'm sorry you lost your leg, Grandpa, but happy you could get a new one. You're lucky to be a boy and always have pants to cover it."

Lars laughs and calls Sven to come over. Sven jumps into his lap, and Lars takes Freyja's hand, asking her to come and play catch in the yard. "Don't worry, Grandma; I'll watch and make sure Grandpa doesn't fall."

I smile and kiss her. "I know you will."

We watch as Lars and Freyja hold hands, followed by an excited puppy. It seems to be a fantasy come true: Lars is throwing a Nerf ball, and Sven is chasing it down, bringing it back to Lars and dropping the prize at his feet each time. Such a normal little moment for an anything-but-normal man.

I go over to them and tell Lars, "I think

you should take the leg off and rest. You have had it on for a long time, and we have a lot coming up in a few days."

He frowns. "Okay, Dr. Arlene. I have learned to listen to doctor's orders." He leans over and picks up Sven to take with him.

"Come on, Grandpa. I'll read you a story; I have lots of books." We go to the downstairs bedroom, and the sleeper sofa is already made up. Lars lies down and whispers to me, "Is it okay for Freyja to see the stump? I don't want to scare her."

"Yes, Lars, the consequences of battle should always be viewed by the young, depositing a memory for adulthood, to avoid war." I tell Freyja to go pick a book; then I get the jeans off Lars and put sweatpants on him; Freyja does not need to see anything else.

She returns and Lars says, "Sit here, little one." Freyja climbs up beside Lars as he pulls the leg of his sweatpants up and releases the straps that hold the leg in place. Freyja gasps as she sees the stump, and she reaches over to touch it. "Oh Grandpa, the cost of war, horrible." Lars hugs her and pushes down his pant leg. She pulls two books from her pile and asks, "What can I read you?" Lars points to one and she begins to read. Lars listens to her soft voice and tells her that she is a gift, a treasured gift. She puts her fingers between the pages and pauses.

"Hush, I want to read this to you, Grandpa." I leave the room, looking back at Lars, Freyja, and Sven curled up together, and decide that I need to get a photo of this. I call Cathryn to come and take a picture on her phone, a Kodak moment if there ever was one. She snaps a picture and hugs me, and we softly close the door.

We head back to the kitchen, and I continue telling her about our Norway trip. The initial problems with wearing the leg and walking too much, the PTSD incident as we were coming home, and our visit with his mom and uncle. "Sorry you didn't have a good trip, Mom, but it was probably good for Lars to confront his limitations again and move on."

"Yes, I think it was. It gave him the courage to realize he could have a normal life with me and be a husband."

"Speaking of husbands, Mom, I asked Dad to come for the wedding. I thought the two Grandpas should meet." I think about it and agree. Two old Marines, both vets during Vietnam, one serving there, the other stateside. One broken and damaged, the other whole and a father of three.

Freyja comes into the room. "Grandma, Grandpa is asleep, and Sven is too."

"Thank you, Freyja." We have a quiet but delicious dinner, and Sean suggests we watch a movie. Everyone agrees, and we end up watching *The Lord of the Rings.* I fall asleep and Cathryn wakes me.

"Mom, Lars wants you."

I get up and go to the bathroom, seeing Lars on the floor, no leg on and unable to get up on his own. Relieved to see that nothing is wrong, I call Sean to help him up, and we get him over to the bed. "What were you trying to do, Lars?"

"I had to pee, and I thought I could just hop to the bathroom and back. I fell, nothing close by to grab for support." I kiss him and tuck him into bed. "Sorry, I was trying not to be so helpless."

"Helpless, Lars? Sometimes you are hopeless"—I smile—"but I love you anyway."

CHAPTER SIXTEEN

The next day we go out for a big breakfast and pick up the flowers for the wedding; Cathryn and I will create a few arrangements to dress the yard for tomorrow. I remind Lars to keep his leg off and that he will have to wear it all day tomorrow.

The girls come into our room with Sven, and he jumps up on the bed. Freyja asks, "Can I finish reading my book with you, Grandpa?"

"I would love to hear you read more, Freyja". We decide he should put his leg back on in case he needs the bathroom. We have the girls leave the room for privacy while I help him get his leg on.

I kiss him and tell him, "Tomorrow you are mine, no escaping."

"Back at you, baby. This pain in the ass will be all yours."

I playfully pull down his sweatpants and kiss his ass. "All mine forever, Lars."

After a low-key evening with the family, we are ready to turn in. I check our clothes for tomorrow—ready for the big day.

We sleep well, and we are both up early. Lars and I shower together, and he presses his erection to me. "How about a quickie?"

I smile and shake my head. "No, save it for tonight. But it better not be quick." He needs his leg on to shave, so I return to our room, retrieve it, and bring his clothes and shoes for the day. Shaved, showered, and dressed, an aging Viking stands before me. I have him go sit and rest while I get dressed, so he goes outside. I check my phone for messages from my sons. I know they will not be here today, but I'm hoping they have left me their love, which they have. "Congratulations, Mom; we love you! Have a wonderful day."

Outside, Cathryn brings Lars some wine and tells him, "The food is almost ready, and Father John is on his way. Another hour and you're officially Grandpa." She clicks on the playlist they have composed and pats his shoulder. The girls meet me downstairs, all of us dressed for the event, and we make our way out to the backyard.

Lars comes over to us. "God, my three beautiful girls." He kisses me and asks where Sven is, and Freyja tells him that her mom thought we should put him in a crate since there will be so many people here.

Father John is here; he and Lars go sit and talk for a few moments, and then it is time, so they make their way over to the gazebo and await my arrival. As I walk to Lars, Cathryn clicks a button, and the soft, lilting voice of Roberta Flack sings "The First Time Ever I Saw Your Face." Lars and I are both in tears as the song finishes, and Father John begins. It is a simple ceremony and ends as we cross ourselves, kiss, and turn to everyone standing and applauding.

We sit down, and Cathryn says, "Don't you want to dance?" I shake my head, and Lars explains that he doesn't want to fall in front of everybody. Father John comes over and says, "Peace be with you both, and may God protect such a special pair." We thank him; then the girls come over with champagne for us and say, "Welcome to our family, Grandpa Lars."

Cathryn brings over Steven, and he tells Lars, "I'm the other grandpa." I introduce the two and explain that he is my ex and the

Katherine Zartman

father of my kids. The former Marines talk for a bit, and Lars stands. Steven moves to shake his hand, and as it becomes a bit awkward with no left hand to shake, he gives Lars a pat on the shoulder instead.

Lars motions me to come with him, and we go to the bathroom. He hugs me fiercely and kisses me deeply. "You are beautiful, baby. And all mine now."

We go back out and have a few more glasses of champagne, then a wonderful dinner, after which Sven runs out and jumps onto Lars's lap. Cathryn brings out an enormous chocolate cake, and soon, we all have chocolate icing on our faces. She pulls me aside and tells me that she and Sean have made a reservation for us at a hotel close by. It is a handicap room on the ground floor for two days, and they will watch Sven. "You go pack, and I'll talk to Lars." I hug her tightly as Steven comes over to us. Cathryn turns to him. "So, Dad, what do you think?"

He smiles his congratulations to me. "I think your mom is still beautiful, and she married a special man." He hugs me and kisses my cheek. "You made a good choice, Arlene; I wish you the best." I thank him, then head inside to pack everything and deposit the bags near the

98

front door. I return to the backyard, and we have a final glass of champagne. The girls hug and kiss Lars; then he gathers me in his arms.

"Any second thoughts?"

"Absolutely not, Grandpa," I say, and then we are off, Cathryn driving us to the hotel.

In our room, Lars falls onto the bed. "Come here, Wife, and make love to me." I go to the bed and help him out of his jeans and then out of his leg. He kisses me deeply as he pulls me on top of him. "I want you slow and easy." We move together, and Lars begins to pant, breathing, "Take me now; let me really feel you." I increase my pace, and he explodes. "I love you, Arlene. I love you."

We cuddle together, content to start the next phase of our life together. We nap for a few hours before Lars needs the bathroom. I grab his now-seldom-used crutch, and we head to the bathroom, where I hold his penis as he pees, just like old times. I turn around to start the shower and notice a large white walk-in tub, the first I have seen in a hotel room. *Thank you, Cathryn; we will enjoy this.* I show Lars and ask, "So, how does a hot bubble bath sound?"

He takes a breath. "Do you think I can get in and out of it?"

"It is a walk-in tub, so hopefully it will be no problem," I respond. I turn on the water, add a generous amount of bubbling bath oil, and guide Lars into the tub and onto the seat. Tossing his crutch to the floor, he leans back, enjoying the warmth and the bubbles. "We should get one of these, baby."

"Yes, we should. I love bubble baths." I sit down in front of him, lower than he is. He reaches forward and caresses my breasts, then ventures down lower and begins to circle his long fingers around my sex.

Softly, he whispers, "Open your legs wider, baby; I want you to come for me." I spread my legs, and he continues to circle his fingers. I lean my head against his right leg and close my eyes, enjoying the warm water and his now-skilled fingers. I feel the pulsing coming, and Lars increases the pressure, telling me to come for him. I pant through my climax and Lars says, "Now, turn around and sit on me."

I turn and take Lars into me as he sucks a breast. I move up and down carefully as I don't want water to spill from the tub. I increase my movement, and Lars is soon panting, "Faster, baby, faster!" before he loudly explodes. Leaning to kiss me, he says, "I think that was our best fuck ever. We have to get one of these tubs! I love you, baby. I love you." I add more hot water, and we just relax, content to just hold each other. *Married, married for life.*

The water cools, so I empty the tub and give Lars his crutch. I admire his body as I dry him off, and I can't resist kissing his ass, prompting him to swat mine. We slip into the bed and fall asleep, clinging to each other.

In the morning, we wake, dress, and go over to the hotel restaurant. Pancakes, eggs, bacon, and coffee—we are hungry as we had no dinner. Returning to our room, we pull our clothes off, experienced newlyweds wanting again to express our love. I pull him to my mouth, hungry for dessert after breakfast. Lars is panting and tells me, "I want to take you hard now, baby." I lie on my back and he covers me, driving his pulsing cock into me as he yells, "Put your hands on my ass and pull me in and out! Harder baby, harder." I increase the pressure on his ass, and he buries his face between my breasts as he comes. "Fuck, fuck, Arlene, you could kill me like this!"

We spend a quiet day and make love again, insatiable in our desire. In a quiet moment, I ask Lars to talk to me. "Tell me about Nam and how you felt then and now." Lars looks at me and says, "A gunner on a Huey, flying into a hot LZ to pick up wounded. Under fire with mortars, and then I felt a sharp pain in my neck," he remembers as he strokes the scar on his neck. "I woke up in a hospital, my leg amputated and no left hand. I wondered how any woman would want me, damaged as I was. How could I hold a woman? How could I walk? I was pissed that the Marines had taken my life, and I would never get it back, while my limbs were in some trash can and my body never to be whole again. I can't talk about this, baby. It just draws me back there. I can smell burning flesh and feel the pain on the flight to the hospital." A few tears leak from his clear, blue eyes, and he turns away from me. "How can you love me, baby, how?"

"Only in every way, Lars, in every way. You know I don't see your missing parts. I only see those blue eyes and your tender heart. A perfect mate for me."

The tears roll down his face, and I draw him to me, hugging him hard. "I hate crying like a baby, Arlene. You make me so emotional."

"Oh Lars, when are you going to realize you are whole and so deeply loved?" I ask.

"I'm almost there, baby. You married me,

you love me, you don't wince when you see me naked."

"No Lars, I'm excited when I see you naked; trust me," I say with a grin.

"Well, baby, get me naked, and we can make love again; I need more convincing that I'm still sexy."

"Yes, sir," I say, and I close my lips around his cock as he sighs.

"At least they left me this."

My sad, tender Viking. What will convince you that your debt is paid in full? I am so overcome with love that I draw him to me and cry on his chest. We have no words; our touch and our connection say everything the other needs to know. Afterward, we are both hungry, so we dress and go to the dining room. Meatloaf and potatoes: comfort food to sooth raw emotions.

CHAPTER SEVENTEEN

We have coffee for breakfast the next day and decide on another hot bath before we have to leave. We get in the bath, and I fill it with hot water and lots of bubbles; no sex this time—just tender touches and deep kissing. An hour later, we dress, and Cathryn comes to take us home. "How was it, Mom?"

"Great. We love the walk-in tub. We plan to look into getting one at home."

Back at her house, we watch the movie *Return of the King* and go to bed early. The next morning, the girls wake and come down to hug and kiss Grandma and Grandpa, Lars still surprised to hear the endearment. We get packed and ready to leave. We hug our goodbyes and thank Cathryn and Sean for everything as she hands us a thermos of coffee.

Twelve long hours and we will be home. Sven curls up on Lars's familiar lap, and we have light traffic getting out of California. We stop for lunch and use the restrooms, then laugh as the long, green grass confuses Sven with its artificial feel.

Finally, home. Home at last. Lars says, "Sorry I can't carry you in."

I kiss him and say, "Just carry Sven." I feed Sven, and he goes out the doggie door, returning shortly to his bed in our room.

Lars takes off his leg and says, "Sorry, baby, I'm too tired tonight."

"I know," I say with a yawn. "I'm tired too; long drive."

We wake at ten the next morning, and Sven has been out and back, now pawing at our bedside, imploring Lars to pick him up. He scoops Sven up, and he curls up immediately on Lars's chest. We have coffee and a hot shower, sleep for a few more hours, and take Sven for a walk. We also call and make an appointment with the lawyer to set up a trust as we are now legal, and we have talked about our wishes and intentions. It will be several days before the trust is established. I go to the grocery store and buy enough for this week and more; then I call and make an appointment with Dr. Todd so that he can check on his progress and the leg.

When we see him, Dr. Todd congratulates us on our marriage, then asks if both of us would be interested in becoming mentors for another PTSD group. "You are perfect to show support much needed by these men." He takes us down to meet the group, and I revert to Nurse Arlene, talking softly and patting shoulders. Dr. Todd explains who we are and what Lars has been through, noting that we are now married.

Lars pulls up his right pant leg and says, "No leg, no hand, and I couldn't stand being around blood. This woman gave me my life back. I'm missing a few parts, but her love for me cancels that deficit." Tearing up, he continues. "You'll see, and we will be back to visit with you and learn your stories."

Dr. Todd thanks us and says, "Lars, you married the best."

"Dr. Todd," he responds, "I married the only one."

We get home, and he brings me into his arms. "Come here, baby. I want to love you and thank you." We make love, and Lars professes his thanks for saving him.

"I paid a high price for the freedom I

fought for. You came along and erased the debt and gave me back everything I lost in Nam. I am whole, proud, and baby, I'm so in love with you." Tears roll down my cheeks. Freedom found.

www.ingramcontent.com/pod-product-compliance
Lightning Source LLC
Chambersburg PA
CBHW051346020726
47501CB00007B/2303